SARAH DYER is the award-winning author and illustrator of
Five Little Fiends, *Mrs Muffly's Monster* and *Batty*.
Monster Day at Work is her sixth book
and she has been published in over nine countries.
Sarah was always very helpful with her dad at work,
and only ate some of the biscuits
at the morning meetings.

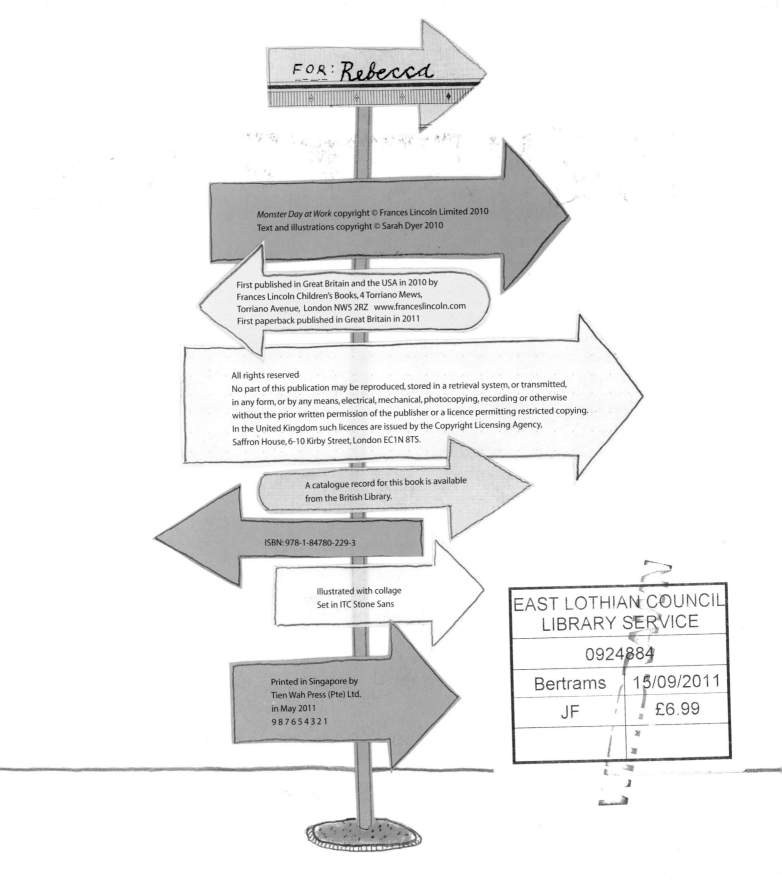

FOR: Rebecca

Monster Day at Work copyright © Frances Lincoln Limited 2010
Text and illustrations copyright © Sarah Dyer 2010

First published in Great Britain and the USA in 2010 by
Frances Lincoln Children's Books, 4 Torriano Mews,
Torriano Avenue, London NW5 2RZ   www.franceslincoln.com
First paperback published in Great Britain in 2011

A catalogue record for this book is available
from the British Library.

ISBN: 978-1-84780-229-3

Illustrated with collage
Set in ITC Stone Sans

Printed in Singapore by
Tien Wah Press (Pte) Ltd.
in May 2011
9 8 7 6 5 4 3 2 1

MONSTER DAY at WORK

Sarah Dyer

F

FRANCES LINCOLN
CHILDREN'S BOOKS

Today Scamp and I are going to work with Dad. I have to do everything Dad does at work.

HWELLO! THERE
MDM

First I have to decide
what to wear.

"Choose me a tie please Scamp.

Ahh . . . lovely choice. Thank you."

Then we have to get to work.

Wow, rush hour really is . . . well, a rush!

The first job is a very important
morning meeting.

1UP:02   HIGH:10

Puter

After the meeting we have to
do some work on the computer.
That is very easy – I get a much
higher score than Dad.

At last it is time for our lunch.

After lunch I colour in the charts Dad has spent all morning working on!

Then we have a nap. Well, I definitely do.
And I'm sure Dad needs one too.

We also visit
the bank.

After work Dad likes to exercise
so we go to the gym.

Then Dad treats me to some drinks.

And Scamp is allowed a biscuit.

Then it is more rush hour on the way home.

I have had a great day. It was all very easy.

I don't know why Dad complains so much,

but I think tomorrow I am going to stay with Mum. . .

Who has it easy too.